Wind Up Hearts

Stan Swanson

Wind Up Hearts

Copyright © Stan Swanson 2017
All Rights Reserved

ISBN: 978-0-9962834-2-7

HELIUM BOOKS
Salina, Kansas

Wind Up Hearts

Stan Swanson

This book is dedicated to those who have had the fortune to find love and to those who might still be searching. Just be thankful our hearts are flesh and blood so Cupid's arrows can still find their mark.

*"We already live a very long time for mammals,
getting three times as many heartbeats as a mouse or elephant.
It never seems enough, though, does it?"*

—David Brin

The Present

The familiar clicking of Henry Thackery's heart made him uneasy this day, and he found himself picking up an old habit of counting the beats. In years past, he would sometimes find himself staring off into space timing the steady rhythm, but he could never make it past a few hundred. He always attributed it to a loss of concentration, but a small part of him was afraid to try and count any higher. He was not typically a superstitious man, but there was nothing typical about the situation. If the old philosophies were true—if man had a finite number of heartbeats predetermined by the fates on the day they were born—then Henry Thackery was an anomaly.

The fates were wrong.

At least in his case.

As he approached the park bench—so familiar after these many years—his stomach stirred. He took a deep breath. The crisp air of an early winter pained his throat and caused his false teeth to chatter. Why did he get so nervous on each occasion of meeting her, even after thousands of times?

And there she was.

She sat there on their park bench as beautiful as the day they had met. Though her hair was now spun silver thread, her green eyes still glittered like emeralds submerged in shining water.

How long had it been? A hundred years? Longer? His mind wasn't as sharp as it had been in his younger days. Some things he remembered; some things he forgot. But he never forgot how he felt each time he encountered her.

She didn't look up from her book, even though her head tilted at the familiar footsteps. Nowadays, they were accompanied by the *clickety-clack* of his metal-tipped cane on the cement walk. But the smile on her lips told him that she knew who was approaching.

The curve of her mouth brought hundreds of memories of that same smile shining at him over steaming plates of roasted turkey at countless Thanksgiving dinners, or beaming above the crumpled balls of gift wrapping paper strewn at their feet on so many Christmas mornings. A hearth-cozy smile like hers might cause a man's heart to swell and beat a little faster. But not Henry's heart. Henry's heart could not swell or beat at a different rate.

"Good morning, Emily," he said, offering the lady a bouquet of freshly arranged white carnations. She had once called them "the flowers of God." Henry wasn't sure what that meant exactly, but he had interpreted it as a good thing.

"Carnations! Thank you, Henry! I swear, if you had continued to bring me roses all these years, you would be in debtor's prison or laboring your life away on the poor farm by now. Well, if there were such things in this day and age."

"Not very likely, my dear," he replied. "I'm careful with my pennies."

She laughed, and his spirit lifted. He thought he would never forget the sweet chime of her voice or the velvety richness of her laughter—no matter what her answer to him might bring this day. No matter what she might say. No matter how she would react.

"Pennies?" she scoffed. "You deal with more than mere pennies, my dear Henry. I imagine you lighting your rank cigars with hundred-dollar bills!"

"Two hundred–dollar bills actually."

She grinned. "There is no such thing as a two-hundred-dollar bill!"

"My dear Emily, have you not considered that the reason you have never seen a two-hundred-dollar bill is because I have simply used them all to light my delightfully aromatic cigars?"

She scowled. "You need to quit smoking, Henry. Haven't you read a newspaper headline for the past three decades? Or even longer! Have you paid no attention to the public warnings about the dangers of inhaling tobacco smoke?"

"Emily, you needn't fret about me. If my cigars haven't killed me by now, they never will."

Her green eyes crinkled at the corners. "I never said I cared if you died," she replied with as straight a face as she could muster. "I just don't delight in the smell of those things as much as you seem to."

He bowed and kissed her gently on the cheek. He was pleased that, in spite of all her protests, she didn't pull away from his sickly-sweet, cigar-scented lips.

She did blush, however.

Even after all these years, some things never changed. And he had come to love that hint of crimson highlighting her face. Using his cane for balance, Henry took his time settling down beside her on the bench. He hated his cane as it seemed to him a sign to all the world of his frailty.

He glanced down the cement walk as he always did when he and Emily visited together on the bench beneath the sycamore. The next bench sat twelve yards farther down the lakefront. Over the decades, he and Emily had seen a variety of couples sitting there, all different in their ways as time flowed on. There had been corseted ladies dutifully ignoring young paramours, young bobby-soxers dancing together on the bench to rockabilly music blasting from a hand-held radio, and even bell-bottomed duos sunning themselves topless as they smoked their funny cigarettes. But today, the bench sat empty.

The cold weather could have had something to do with the vacant benches. Winter had crept into the city like shadows in the twilight, sneaking in unnoticed until one finally realizes that everything is in darkness. Henry leaned his cane against the bench and placed his large hand over Emily's smaller one. The warmth of her skin radiated into his palm.

"Did you bring your key?" he asked.

"Of course, I have my key," she replied, a mild hint of irritation edging her voice. She had forgotten her key only once, many years ago. "But must we do it now? I'd like to sit and talk for a while if you don't mind. We have plenty of time."

Henry wasn't much of a talker, but considered himself a great listener. Emily seemed to enjoy how well he listened, although she encouraged him to talk more often, especially when she knew something was bothering him. He usually confided in her when all was said and done, but it wasn't an easy task for her to drag it out of him. "Certainly, my dear. There's no hurry."

He glanced down at the book nestled in her lap. "What are you reading this week? Another romance?"

She pouted. He expected no less. This teasing was simply another element in their routine. "Now, Henry, I don't read romance novels every day of the week! I like a good mystery now and then, and you know I love my science fiction and gothic horror—"

"And tales of suspense, of monsters and mayhem, of machines and magic. Yes, I am quite aware of your taste in reading material by now," he said with a devilish grin.

She hesitated. "But, yes, this one is a romance."

"Are you enjoying it?"

"Yes, but I must admit I am still uneasy with some of the language they use now. I picked up a new book two days ago, and it was so explicit! I couldn't get through a single chapter without feeling myself grow red in the face." She averted her eyes, still a bit uncomfortable with such talk even after all these years.

"And was that book also a romance novel?"

"Yes, although a little more, shall we say, sensual. And I hear that sensual romances are very big sellers. Full of, well, throbbing and, uh, trembling."

He cocked one eyebrow.

"And they are written for women?"

"Yes, and by women for the most part. Guess it's a different generation. I remember when women couldn't go near a voting booth, and now they're so, well, scandalous in their writing."

"Sounds like these books are pure pornography to me," he scoffed.

"Like you haven't read a *Playboy* or two in your time, Mr. Henry Thackery. Or watched a blue movie." She swiped a finger playfully across his cheek.

"Not in quite some time, my dear," he murmured with a pinch of disappointment in his voice. "Besides, just as you say, it is a different generation."

He glanced to his left, toward the busy street that ran along the east edge of the park. She followed his gaze, and they sat there, watching the traffic as the cool air from the lake curled in around them. Suddenly, Emily raised her right arm and pointed toward the road, nearly smacking Henry's face in the process.

"Look! There's the new Ford!" she shouted into his right ear. Thirty years ago he might have winced, but his hearing was nearly gone now on that side, and it wasn't much more acute in his other ear. He nodded and feigned interest. Henry had never owned a car. Well, that wasn't quite true. He'd owned dozens and dozens of cars.

Stan Swanson

He had simply never learned to drive. It had never been necessary for him to drive anywhere.

Emily pointed again. "Remember when that boutique there on the corner used to be a soda fountain? When did it close? 1950?"

He smiled. He did remember. "Best cherry colas in town," he whispered as he took her hand in his.

She nodded, and their fingers intertwined.

They sat there quietly for quite some time, and it made Henry uneasy. Emily was usually very talkative. Except when something bothered her.

He fidgeted on the bench. It was still strange to be in a stressful situation and not feel the increase in the rate of heartbeats.

"You should have told me sooner, Henry. I deserved to know," she said in a soft voice.

He sighed, remembering how she'd looked the first day he'd seen her so long ago. "I know, Emily," he said quietly. "I'm sorry."

A single snowflake fell, gracing the back of Emily's hand. It lighted there, white and crystalline for a moment, before it melted and rolled down her finger with the slow ease of a tear. They were so lost in reflection that neither of them noticed.

1875

An invigorating breeze from the lake etched away at the warmth of an early spring day as trees discovered new buds, flowers debated waking from winter's sleep, and love sauntered along the sidewalks of the bustling city, looking for new clients.

Henry's shuffling gait was much slower than it should have been for a young man in his mid-twenties. Taking deep breaths was painful. That could have simply been an after effect of the surgery. After all, it had only been a week. But he supposed skittish nerves also slowed his progress.

The more he thought about the prospect of seeing the woman on the park bench—a book perched in her lap and a parasol protecting her from the sunny afternoon—the more his gait increased, regardless of the pain that blossomed beneath his rib cage.

He put his hand against the thick bandages covering his chest and hoped their bulk was not evident under his clothing.

There she was.

Her auburn hair was pulled into a bun and secured with a mother-of pearl comb. The skirt of her blue and white gingham dress billowed neatly around her knees. She was beautiful.

At the sight of her, he remembered that very first day he'd seen her. Even all of those decades could not erase that memory. That had been the day she had received the news, he suspected.

That had been the day he had fallen in love with her.

Her face had not been so calm and cool then. The skin around her mouth had been tight and pale and her eyes downcast. She had walked that day with an almost indiscernible slump, as if her hands were filled with parcels even though they were empty. He was glad to see that now she seemed to have fully recovered from her procedure, and though he was not a religious man, Henry thanked the skies above. Where so many others had floundered and failed to thrive, she was strong, and he was grateful beyond words.

And even though his prayers for her health and well-being filled his thoughts, he knew that she didn't even know he existed. At least, not yet.

If only his courage could hold out, he hoped that would soon change. But a knot of fear had worked its way up Henry's throat. He was a man who could devour high-level businessmen and entrepreneurs in a single gulp at a boardroom meeting. He could stare them down with the cold steel of his eyes until they broke and looked away. All his young life, he had felt that he could stand up to anyone or anything, and make any demand.

But in her presence, he was powerless. She was different.

She absent-mindedly twirled the white parasol above her head as she turned another page in her book, unaware of the effect she was having on the young man who stiffly approached her.

Henry's mouth went dry, and his hand involuntarily rose to touch his chest again. His surgeons would have thrown a fit if they knew that he had dressed and left the hospital. His only obstacle had been an orderly, but a wad of bills quickly convinced the young fellow to allow Henry to do as he pleased. He simply had to see her.

Henry knew that the young seamstress in the blue and white dress was named Emily and that she left her small shop on the opposite side of the park and took her mid-day meal here every day. Even when it rained, she came, carrying her cloth-swaddled lunch. Henry had waited long enough as he stood at the end of the gravel path and pretended to read his newspaper. He had thought of little else over the past dozen weeks, and it was all that had kept him managing the pain following the surgery.

He wondered if her scar still bothered her, as well. He reasoned that the mark on her chest must be similar to his in length and size, but he imagined hers as a work of art settled beautifully between her perfectly shaped breasts. He wondered if the ragged mark still caused her discomfort at times and if she also resisted the urge to scratch at the itch that accompanied the healing process. His own, more recent scar often drove him crazy, but of course, she had undergone her surgery weeks before.

Henry took a deep breath to steel himself, but the effort tugged at his incision. He winced, but his heart never skipped a beat.

And it never would.

Straightening his coat, Henry buttoned his vest. The fabric rubbed against his bandage, but one should never approach a lady if not properly dressed. Even a lurid lady of the night would likely turn and run the other way if a man had wandered up to them with an open jacket and no tie. First impressions were important.

He shuffled along slowly, trying to appear not quite so much an invalid. He paused near the bench, and Emily glanced up briefly from her book to determine what had cast a shadow over the words she was reading.

He tipped his new Parisian top hat and stretched his mouth into the widest smile he could manage. He knew how gaunt he must look after his surgery, and he worried she might see nothing but his pale skin, sunken cheeks, and the sallow circles beneath his eyes. He imagined himself grinning toothily down at her as only a madman could.

If she gets up and rushes away, he thought nervously, *it will end before it begins*. There was no way he would be able to run after her to explain his conduct. Their relationship would be over before it had a chance to develop. And though he knew it would be scientifically impossible, he worried his heart might break.

"May I?" he asked, indicating the space on the bench beside her. His hand shook, and he tried to steady it as he met her eyes.

Barely seeming to notice him, she shrugged and glanced

momentarily at gulls that were diving for things only they could see beneath the lake's surface, then returned her attention to her book.

So much for first impressions, he thought ruefully.

"Lovely day," he finally sputtered after suffering several moments of agonizing silence.

She simply nodded and turned another page.

Henry's anxiety increased. His intake of breath came quicker, and he swallowed, though his mouth was dry as an old, empty icebox. His heart, though, ticked steadily. The cowardly part of him, which was small but rather vocal, wanted to mumble a simple good afternoon and shuffle back to the hospital. Nothing threatening there except doctors with sharp scalpels and nurses with pointy needles. Much less terrifying than this, surely.

He cleared his throat. "Do you perchance have the time of day?" Without looking up, she shook her head.

"Do you perchance possess the faculties required for human speech?" He spoke without thought and immediately regretted his quip. He knew if he was too forward, too familiar, it could end everything. With rising panic, he tried to appear calm and nonchalant.

She looked up from her book, blinked, and turned her gaze upon him as if finally noticing his presence. Under a knitted brow, she scrutinized him for a moment as if inspecting his face for a spot of muck or a sign of evil. After a moment, her face smoothed. A smile followed, and from that point, Henry's day brightened substantially.

"I'm sorry, sir," Emily said. "I am entirely too engrossed in my reading, and it was terribly impolite of me to ignore you so. I am usually not so inadequate in the ways of etiquette."

"No need to apologize. I've always thought that one must lose oneself now and again."

"Are you poking fun at me, sir?" she asked. "Or are you simply flirting?" Now he was flustered.

He opened his mouth and then closed it. He had no idea how to respond, so he said nothing. In any case, her smile alone had the ability to still his voice in his throat and every other muscle in his body. Well, maybe not every muscle...

She came to his rescue. "Emily Harding," she said rather formally, extending her hand.

He gently took it for one brief moment, gripping the fingers lightly with his own. He was careful not to be overly forward, though he ached at the thought of turning her hand palm down and pulling it gently to his mouth.

"Henry Thackery," he responded.

A racket on the nearby thoroughfare interrupted their brief conversation. "Oh, how grand!" she said, raising her hand to her cheek as she gazed with wide eyes toward the street.

His eyebrows rose. "What the devil?"

"Mr. Thackery. Watch your language!"

He glanced at her, confused by the grin on her face. Was she teasing him, or had his language truly offended her? Was she simply being polite and trying to make him comfortable, or was she chastising him as a straitlaced governess might? He sighed. No wonder the urge to settle down with a woman had not been a priority in his younger life. They were, well—just too complex.

"Look at it!" she said with a grand gesture at the vehicle chugging down the street. "It's one of those newfangled steam-driven automobiles! Isn't it marvelous?"

Henry shrugged. "I suppose, but give me a good old horse and buggy any day of the week. All that noise and commotion! How can one possibly ponder the meaning of life amid that infernal racket?"

"There goes your language again, Mr. Thackery. Are you trying to upset me?" She grinned—mischievously, he thought—though he wasn't sure.

"Hell no, ma'am," he said softly with emphasis on the word *hell*.

Her grin didn't fade, but she blushed just the same.

The steam-powered contraption chugged off, leaving them in relative peace and quiet.

"Technology isn't always a good thing, Miss Harding. You just watch. One day it will cost men their jobs."

"Possibly," she replied. "But you can no more stop the advance of technology than you can the spinning of the earth. We shan't always be riding in horse-drawn buggies, Mr. Thackery."

I don't know why you think so, he thought to himself, choosing not to voice his opinion. He understood the irony of his viewpoint. If not for the advance of technology, he would not be sitting here, engaging the beautiful Emily Harding in conversation.

"What are you reading?" he asked.

"Oh, this?" She held up her volume. "It is a novel by Jules Verne. *Le Tour du Monde en Quatre-Vingts Jours*," she stated matter-of-factly, her French accent indiscernible from that of the shopkeepers whose shops he had occasioned on his visits to Paris. "He is a wonderful writer! Such an imagination!"

"You are reading it in French?" he asked.

She nodded. "Yes. I understand that it has been translated into English, but I prefer to read it in the language in which it was written. Things are often lost in translation. Don't you agree?" Henry looked at her blankly.

"Have you read Monsieur Verne?" she asked when she received no answer.

"I do not read much outside of newspapers and financial journals. Life is too short for frivolity."

He realized the mockery of the statement the moment it left his lips.

"So you feel I waste my life by reading books and educating myself?" This time, her eyes did not twinkle.

"No, certainly not. I did not mean to imply any such thing, Miss Harding! Please forgive my thoughtlessness."

"But you are able to read, are you not?" she chided. "I mean, you know how to spell cat and dog, naturally?"

"Of course I can read," he huffed, trying to keep his voice from betraying his nervousness. "I just have more important things to do with my time."

"Such as flirting with strange women in the park?"

His response was immediate. "Only if they are beautiful."

The flattery caught her off guard and seemed to unsettle her, but only momentarily. "I will take that as a compliment, Mr. Thackery, though I think it a bit forward on your part."

Henry started to reply, but as he took a breath, he winced.

"Are you in pain, Mr. Thackery?" she asked with what felt like genuine concern.

The truth was, Henry was not feeling well. Not that he would ever admit it to her. He didn't want this moment with her to end. His body, however, was telling him a different tale. It was time to return to the hospital.

"I am fine, thank you, Miss Harding."

"Why do you call me *Miss* Harding?"

"I am sorry. Are you married?" he asked, suddenly unsure of himself. Though he had never seen her with a man and he saw no golden band around the finger of her left hand, what if his assumptions had been wrong? What if she had a husband secreted away in the crawlspace above her shop? What if he lived bound to an invalid's chair, unable to speak, totally dependent on her, and she loved him, still? Henry feared his belief in her availability might have been a presumption that would crush him. Suddenly speechless with worry, he chewed the inside of his lip as he looked at her.

Her gaze lifted to the lake, her mood seeming to decline. He did not like the change. He wanted to see her happy forever.

"I am a widow, Mr. Thackery," she replied in a distant voice. "My husband died of pneumonia nearly two years ago."

"I must offer you my deepest condolences, then, Madame. I apologize for, well, *Mrs.* Harding it is, then."

She shrugged, and some of the darkness seemed to slip from her shoulders. "Life comes, and it goes. It is such a fragile thing."

More than anything, he knew just how fragile. He longed to take her in his arms and pull her close. He did not, of course. Instead, he reached inside his vest for his pocket watch. As he pulled it free by its gold chain, something fell, clinking to the cobblestone beneath their feet. He retrieved it quickly but saw the look of recognition that covered her face. She unconsciously moved a hand between the swell of her breasts to clasp the similar key that hung from a silver chain about her neck.

Emily gazed at the small, ornate key on her chain, then at the one in Henry's fingers.

She rose quickly.

"I must be going, Mr. Thackery," she said, placing her book into her satchel. She turned so abruptly to walk away that he was unable to utter a single goodbye. Henry wanted to call out to her as she walked away, but he did not. His body sagged against the back of the wooden bench. If it could have, his heart would have slumped lifeless in his chest. But, of course, it couldn't.

The Present

Henry sat quietly on the bench next to Emily. "*Un sou pour vos pensées*?" Emily asked as a snowflake came to rest beneath an emerald-green eye. It melted quickly against the warmth of her cheek. Henry brushed the wetness away with the tip of his finger and smiled.

"I was thinking about the past," he replied. "And now you owe me a penny."

He had learned more than a few French words over the last dozen decades with Emily. He would, however, never be up to her task of reading Jules Verne in the original French as she did, and had no desire to ever do so.

"The past?" she inquired.

He wanted to tell her how he regretted not spending every day of his life at her side. He wanted to tell her how he wished things had been different between them, how he wished she had agreed so long ago, but he did not. "It is nothing. Just the fleeting thoughts of an old man."

He studied the bouquet of carnations she held in her hand. "Perhaps next week I'll bring you roses."

"Next week is an eternity away, Henry," she said softly. "And why would you bring me roses? You know I don't want them. They're too expensive. You've brought me beautiful carnations for decades, and I've probably saved you thousands of dollars."

"Roses are the flower that signify love, Emily." She was quiet for a moment.

"I like carnations," she said. "Even a simple bouquet of daisies or pansies is a thing of beauty."

"But daisies and pansies don't express my feelings for you, Emily."

She turned away from his gaze and pretended to be interested in a flock of geese sailing over the choppy waters of the lake.

"I love you," he said softly.

"I know you do, Henry. You've told me every week for over a century now."

"Does that mean you want me to stop telling you?"

She clasped his hand tighter. "My stomach says it is time for lunch, dear Henry. What lovely delight have you brought to tingle my palette?"

"It's not your palette I'd like to tingle," he said, a sly grin on his face.

"Mr. Thackery!" she gasped with a practiced swoon. Henry laughed and held up a grease-soaked paper bag.

"Hot dogs with all the fixin's and chili cheese fries! I do so love this modern cuisine."

She shook her head. "Are you trying to kill me, *mon ami*?"

"Never!" he exclaimed as if wounded. "Besides, your heart is impervious to this stuff."

"My heart, perhaps," she conceded. "But I still have arteries to be clogged."

"Hey, we all have to go sometime."

She was quiet for several minutes as she sampled a few of the fries. They were delicious as usual. His hot dog was half-gone before she had even unwrapped her own.

He spoke through a mouthful of fries. "Remember when that shop on the corner use to be a soda fountain?"

Emily paused and studied him. "We conversed about that just a few minutes ago, Henry. Are you sure you're feeling all right?"

"I'm fine," he said with a nonchalant tone. But it bothered him that he didn't remember her saying that. Maybe he had been distracted, admiring her legs or her chest. Even though she was nearing 150 years old, her breasts were still quite shapely. Time had treated her well.

And her heart, her unbreakable heart, ticked as strongly as ever.

1875

Henry shielded his eyes from the sun reflecting off the lake. In spite of a barrage of threats from his doctors, he had taken leave of the hospital again. There were more important matters on his mind than healing from his surgery.

"My heart is fine," he had informed them.

"Of course the mechanism is fine," was their response. "We're not worried about the mechanism. It either works after the implant or it doesn't. At whatever point you die, Mr. Thackery, it will not be because of your heart. It will be because you have allowed yourself to be overtaken by infection or pneumonia. There are other parts of your body which are, forgive us, less indestructible than your heart."

Henry did not care.

He limped along, a bouquet of white lilies from the hospital gift shop in one hand and a cigar in the other. *My doctors will not be too happy about the cigar, either*, he thought. Nor the glass of wine he'd imbibed across the street to steady his nerves. It hadn't helped much. The butterflies in his stomach had turned from beautiful winged creatures to hungry little monsters, nibbling at his innards.

He glanced at the lilies clutched in his hand with a sigh. He had wanted to buy her roses, the flowers of love, but there were none to be had so early in the season. *Lilies will have to do,* he thought. *Though I'm not sure what they symbolize, I hope it is something eternal and romantic.*

At that moment, he rounded the path by the lake and lifted his gaze toward the bench.

But his trek was for naught.

The park bench sat empty in the soft sun of the early spring. Henry sat down to wait, finished his cigar, and an hour later tossed the already wilting lilies behind a bush. With a rub of weary eyes, he began the journey back to the hospital. His heart ticked away, but Henry felt as if something inside had broken. Not the brassy gear-like wheels which wound and whirred together nor the tiny watch plate springs that held the contraption taught in his chest, but something deeper and more tender. His spirit, he thought. Or perhaps, his very soul.

Clouds had gathered. Henry hadn't bothered to bring an umbrella. And when it started to rain, he didn't care. Men didn't usually die from the common cold. At least, not healthy men with good, strong hearts.

The Present

Absently, Henry stroked his fingertips over his chest, thumbing the edge of his wallet that bulged beneath his jacket. His mind wandered to the ancient and faded duotone of Emily Harding that he kept within it, always near his heart. He had many photograph albums with pages crammed with pictures of the woman who had inspired him, but this particular photo spoke to the depths of his heart, beating as strong today as when he had first received it.

He kept this photograph to remind him how close he had come to losing her that day.

1875

He had brought no flowers to the park the third day as he had expected to find the park bench vacant.

In fact, he was so surprised to see her there that when he rounded the curve in the gravel path, he halted in midstep, painfully pulling at his stitches. Her auburn hair sparkled with the rays of the midday sun.

She glanced up at him.

He tipped his top hat, acting as nonchalantly as possible under the circumstances.

"May I?" he asked, gesturing to the empty spot on the bench.

"Of course," she said.

Her voice was soft and nearly lost in the chirp of the birds and the chatter of the squirrels that went about their routine, unaware and uncaring of any problems outside their own universe. If the earth were flat or round, these tiny creatures never debated. The possible invasion of a crow or two was of much more concern to them.

Henry and Emily sat quietly for a long time, she not talking and he not knowing what to say.

He found himself staring at a young couple who had greeted each other in the park moments earlier. Their embrace seemed overly amorous for such a public place, but they appeared unconcerned. The couple had seated themselves at a park bench farther down the path, the young man's arm firmly around the girl's small waist. The girl giggled as her admirer whispered in her ear.

Henry glanced at Emily, who, thank goodness, seemed not to have noticed them. Her concentration was elsewhere. When she finally spoke, she uttered her words quickly as if she might not otherwise be able to speak them.

"I want to apologize for not being there the other day. I hope you weren't waiting in this weather. It just took me some time to think about things."

"There is nothing to apologize for," he replied.

Emily absent-mindedly twisted the chain about her neck, causing the key to spin slowly between her breasts, which were evident even beneath her blue cotton dress.

She caught him staring, seemingly mesmerized by the action, and her fingers froze. She discreetly tucked the key down the front of her dress and pulled her wool winter coat about her. She blushed when his gaze lingered there even after the silver metal had completed its disappearing act.

Henry forced himself to look away. His gaze wandered back to the couple embracing on the next park bench. He felt somewhat of a voyeur, but found it hard to look away.

"When did you get yours?" asked Emily.

He knew what she was talking about, but pretended ignorance. He looked at her, one eyebrow raised. "Excuse me?"

"Your key," she said. "To your—your heart."

He did not answer directly, frankly not knowing how he should respond. He decided to avoid the question entirely for the moment. "I did not expect to see you here today." He pulled his key from its resting place in his vest pocket, rolling it between his fingers.

"I could not stay away, considering the circumstances," she replied, a catch in her voice. "We may be strangers in this world, but it appears that you and I have a unique bond. I am certain you know to what I am referring. I cannot ignore that most uncommon connection. To my knowledge, there are few of us. Survivors, that is. I must ask you, Mr. Thackery, is it fate that brought us together in this park, or mere coincidence, or something more?"

Henry stroked his perfectly groomed beard.

"I don't believe in coincidence," he said.

"Coincidence. Fate. Maybe it is the same thing. But that being said, you failed to answer my original question. When did you receive your heart?"

"A little over a week ago," he replied.

She spoke, alarm filling her voice. "And you are out and about? Is that wise? I cannot believe your doctors allowed this! They admonished me not to rise from my bed for a week, and I was not permitted to leave the hospital for nearly a month!"

He laughed. "Believe me, my dear lady. My physicians are not aware that I have left the premises. I assure you, they will be furious when they find out."

"How...how do you feel?"

"Stronger every day. And stronger every time I see your face."

She blushed. "Are you being forward again, Mr. Thackery?"

"Please. Call me Henry."

"Not yet, *Mister* Thackery," she replied. "Regardless of our strange connection, we hardly know each other." She hastened another glance at the neighboring park bench. "*Some* people still follow polite decorum in social situations."

He glanced in the direction of the demonstrative couple and watched as the young man ran his fingers lightly along the young lady's leg. The woman allowed it to linger for a moment before she pushed it away with a sly smile.

Henry laughed. "So it seems."

Emily smiled, then turned away to give the couple their privacy. She confused him. She seemed puritanical one moment, but at other times revealed a hint of coquettishness. A curious creature she was. Did he fully understand what he was getting himself in to?

"Are you a well-off man, Mr. Thackery?"

The question caught him off guard.

"What?"

"It is a simple question."

"Now who's being forward?"

"I want to know. You wear expensive clothes. You carry a gold pocket watch. And you were able to afford an extremely expensive medical procedure."

He sighed. "I am—well situated," he finally answered.

She nodded.

"Then, since you are a wealthy man, I can assume you are not interested in my meager life savings. That bodes in your favor, by the way. But now I am beginning to wonder if it was fate, after all, that brought us together. Did the doctors tell you I had the same surgery as yourself? If so, they should be admonished for giving out such private information. You see, I could not afford such an expensive procedure. Could it be that I was simply lucky enough to be chosen as a guinea pig to see if such an expensive operation could be useful for important, wealthy men such as yourself? What else could explain it? To my knowledge, we are the only two people on the Eastern Seaboard with a Merganthol Circulatory Assistance Device implant."

He did not take pleasure from the direction the conversation seemed to be headed. He shifted in his seat. "The devices are a bit pricey, I'll admit, but then again, it is not an item you will find within the pages of the Montgomery Ward catalog."

"That is exactly my point, Mr. Thackery."

"Forgive my obtuseness, my dear, but I'm afraid I do not follow."

"Isn't it apparent? Do I not wear plain dress? Is my parasol not worn and tattered?"

He stared at her blankly.

She sighed. "I am not a rich woman, Mr. Thackery. My deceased husband left me just enough funds to open a small seamstress shop across the way. I earn only enough money to keep my daughter and myself in food and the creditors away from my door."

Henry reached into his coat pocket, pulled out a white baker's bag, and after opening it, offered it to her.

"Gumdrop?" he asked.

She ignored the gesture. "I find it strange, Mr. Thackery."

"You find it strange that I carry gumdrops in my coat pocket? They are in a paper sack, of course. I don't just leave loose candies to tumble about amid my pocket lint, mind you."

"Well, all that might seem a little strange as well, but what I find stranger is the fact you do not ask how I managed to obtain a wind-up heart when I make such a paltry living."

"A wind-up heart? Is that what you call it? I would think that something costing over a hundred thousand dollars deserves to be referred to by its proper name—the Merganthol Circulatory...ah... thingamabob-gadget thingy..."

She smiled. "See? You can't even remember what it is called! Does the device not take the place of the heart?"

"Of course."

"And is it not constructed of gears, springs, regulators, and requires winding?"

"Actually, it has a singular regulator, and the gears are actually wheels, but—yes, you have the basics of it. It is very clocklike in its mechanisms."

"Well, then, a hundred-thousand-dollar device it may be, but it is still simply a wind-up heart."

Henry thought about continuing the debate when he noticed the deliciously playful smile on her lips. "As you wish, my lady. A wind-up heart it is."

"And, as it stands, Mr. Thackery, you have still failed to answer my original question."

"I didn't hear a question in your dissertation," Henry replied, reaching into his bag of gum drops again.

"Don't you find it curious how a woman of little wealth and status might have acquired such a miraculous device?"

"Would not a lady such as yourself find it terribly forward, perhaps even presumptuous of a strange man whose acquaintance she has only recently made, to ask about her financial situation, Mrs. Harding?"

She scowled at him. "It is not fair to answer one question with another, Mr. Thackery."

"Now that I think about it, it could be possible you found your heart lying on the sidewalk. Or perhaps you purloined it from a drunkard in an alley somewhere."

Her scowl disappeared, and she laughed, a welcome twinkle returning to her eye.

"Do I look like a common thief, Mr. Thackery? To say nothing of the fact that a mere seamstress hardly has the skills necessary to implant a mechanical heart. Besides, thieves are after things like gold and silver. People don't go around stealing hearts."

"I disagree, my lady. For you have certainly stolen mine."

The Present

The realization had dawned on Henry that he had been deeply in love for over a century now. If his mechanical heart could flutter at the sight of his true love, it would simply fly from his chest like a bird, young and wild. His muscles might constantly ache and his bones might be old and brittle, but he felt as if he could live forever—as long as Emily was in his life.

He finished his hot dog and his chili cheese fries quickly followed. He then promptly finished the balance of Emily's meal, which she had hardly touched. "I'm sorry," he said, wiping his face with a paper napkin. "Next time I'll bring something you might find more delectable."

"That's what you said the last time," she chided. "I spent hours preparing our lunch last week."

"Hours? You spent hours preparing a Rueben sandwich?"

"Well, perhaps not hours, but you have to admit it was a great sandwich."

He nodded. "Yes, it was."

They listened to a squirrel chatter at them for a moment, then watched as it scampered up a huge, old sycamore tree.

"Remember when they planted that tree?" Emily asked.

He didn't want to admit it, but he did not remember the occasion at all.

"Quite some time ago," he ventured.

"Nearly a hundred years," she replied. "Nearly twenty-five years after we met. The park crew arrived with it in a horse-drawn wagon, and you and I watched together as they hoisted spades full of earth onto the grass to put the tender sapling into the ground. Remember? I said something about how its roots would push through the rough burlap sack that they had packed them into, and you couldn't imagine how a tree could grow so strongly as to break the seams of a sack?"

And, he did almost remember.

"I buried my first heart under a tree," he said, reminiscing. "Well, not me exactly, but my butler, Gregory, took the old organ from the iron box the doctors sent it home in and buried it for me. At the base of an oak tree in my garden. He thought it would keep me strong, I think. Silly, old fool."

"I buried my first heart, too," said Emily softly. "At the base of my husband's memorial stone." She glanced at him and quickly straightened on the bench. "It was so soon after his passing, you see. And I missed him so at times. At least his companionship."

"Naturally," said Henry with a nod while the wheels of his heart turned uninterrupted in spite of the pang of irrational jealousy that shot through his chest.

1900

"Did you bring your key?" Henry asked as Emily opened the wicker picnic basket. The aroma of fried chicken tickled his taste buds.

"You ask me the same thing every week, Henry."

"Yes, I do. And you know why."

Three years earlier she had left her key on the washbasin after her weekly bath and had forgotten to put the chain back around her neck. She hadn't realized it was missing until she reached the park, and they both had rushed back to her flat to retrieve it.

One of the major drawbacks to the mechanical heart was that it needed regular winding like the grandfather clock that stood in his study. The heart could only be wound once a week, and there was but a three-hour window in which that could be accomplished. Henry had been warned many times over that winding the heart too soon could result in the mainspring locking in place, bringing almost instant death. If it were not wound at all, the circulatory process slowed down, resulting in sleepiness and then death as the heart ticked to a stop.

At the time she had misplaced her key, her physicians had suggested that she schedule weekly appointments to act as a reminder to maintain the winding schedule. She could not, of course, afford the weekly visits, although Henry had offered to pay for them. They had finally made a pact to make their heart windings an element of their weekly lunches together.

"And what did I tell you after that harrowing day that you mislaid your key?"

"Well, it wasn't all that harrowing, Henry! And I certainly wasn't going to invite you into my flat every bath day," she replied with a blush. "And I wish you would refrain from talking about me bathing.

It isn't appropriate to allude to one's unclothed body. And with good reason! This aging body might be the one thing that could shock your heart into permanent failure."

"The only thing you could possibly do to my heart is melt it," he said. "You will always be young to me, Emily. You will always be beautiful."

She handed him a napkin and a chicken leg. "Eat," she demanded. "Perhaps a mouthful of food will prevent crazy words from slipping through your lips. You know—I think you used to listen more and talk less."

He leaned over, kissing her lightly on the cheek.

"Mind your manners, Henry! It is the middle of day!"

"Consider it payment for the fine lunch you have prepared."

"So, now you're saying my fried chicken is worth nothing more than a simple kiss on the cheek?" He knew she regretted the words the moment they left her mouth.

"You demand greater reward?" he asked, almost giddily. He moved his lips toward hers, and she promptly stuffed the chicken leg into his mouth.

She grinned. "You are a cad, Mr. Thackery!"

He shrugged and went to work on the fried chicken as she filled a plate with potato salad.

"New hat?" she asked after a few bites.

He removed the hat from his head, holding it out for her inspection.

"It's a bowler. Ordered it from London two months ago. Do you like it?"

She shrugged. "I liked your top hat, better."

"That's not really the style for a gentleman these days, darling," he informed her.

"A top hat will never go out of style, Henry, and please, stop addressing me as 'darling' in public!"

He took her hand, and she did not draw away.

"Emily," he began. She lifted her eyes to his. "I love you."

She sighed. "Henry."

She squeezed his hand, and they finished their meal in silence.

Quietly, they watched as two uniformed park employees pulled up in a wagon and unloaded a sapling from the rear of the wagon bed. They took their time digging, enjoying several cigarettes as they talked more than they worked. They placed the sapling in its new home, sharing a drink from a flask before heading for their next destination.

"Sycamore," Henry said, pulling a cigar from his coat pocket.

"Sycamore? Is that the name of your newest brand of cigar? Where did this one come from? Cuba? Ethiopia? Timbuktu or some other remote country halfway across the world where shipping in a box of smelly cigars costs a thousand dollars?"

"I was talking about the tree those gentlemen just planted. It's a sycamore."

She glanced at the newly planted tree, already drooping in the summer heat as it struggled to adjust to its new surroundings. "Oh," she said. "I've always found it amazing how the roots can push through that sack they are all bound up in."

"I suppose trees are much stronger than people," Henry said. He cocked an eyebrow and leaned forward. "And just so you know, my dear Emily, this cigar cost me a whole nickel over at Delman's Drugstore." He cut off the end of the cigar but did not light it. Instead, he pulled out his pocket watch.

"Almost time for us to return to making a living, Emily Harding." He withdrew his key from his inside vest pocket. "Will you do me the favor?"

"What? Are you an invalid now? Crippled, perhaps?"

"Yes. My heart is crippled. You break it every time you reject my proposals."

"Henry Thackery! Do not think you can make me feel guilty? You are a charming man and very dear to me, but I have my reasons for not marrying. And don't be so vain as to think they have anything to do with you." She crossed her arms haughtily over her chest.

"Indeed, so you have said each and every time I offer myself to you. I daresay, Emily dearest, that these reasons of yours betray any sense of *reason* I can comprehend," Henry said, his voice a little harsher than he'd intended.

She fixed him with an icy glare before turning to feign interest in the newly planted sapling. "It is not your place to understand, Henry. It is simply your place to accept it and move on."

"I wish you could just tell me, dearest, how or what I could do to make you love me." He sighed.

Her expression softened as her gaze fell to the ground in front of her. He thought he could see tears forming in her eyes, but nothing spilled down her smooth cheeks. She opened her mouth to speak, then closed it as if she thought better of it. After a moment, she looked at him and said in a soft voice, "Besides, your heart can never break. It's constructed out of metal."

"They removed the mechanical heart from market last week, you know," Henry informed her resignedly.

"I had read somewhere that the number of people failing to survive the procedure was high, but I hadn't heard the surgery was no longer being performed."

"Well, I think you could say that the death of most of the recipients made it a logical decision."

"And yet here we sit," she mused. "Were we just lucky then?"

"Maybe so, but I'll take luck over chance any day of the week. Otherwise, we both would have been six feet under a long time ago."

She sighed. "I know. I feel guilty sometimes. Not only was I one of the few survivors, I also never found out who paid for my procedure. It would have been nice to be able to thank them. I was assured by the hospital that I was not a guinea pig, although, maybe they just said that to avoid a lawsuit. But they said they couldn't inform me of my benefactor."

"You shouldn't feel guilty, Emily. It was obviously a gift. Just accept it. What you *should* really feel guilty about is your constant failure to accept my hand in marriage."

She slowly turned her head toward Henry again, but he could not quite figure out what the expression on her face meant..

"Oh, look!" She pointed her finger in the direction of a passing streetcar. She cast a sideways glance at Henry to be sure his gaze had fixed in that direction before continuing. "It's one of those new electric cars! Oh, how I would love to drive one of those."

"You said the same thing about steam-powered contraptions. They are all death traps as far as I'm concerned. One of them crashed into a lake in New Jersey last week."

"Was anyone hurt?" she asked with some alarm.

"I don't recall. But it wouldn't surprise me."

He reached out and dropped his key into her hand.

He undid a single button on his white linen shirt, revealing a shiny gold disk inset in the center of his chest. It looked like a tiny, gilded *Alice in Wonderland* portal to the center of his body. The skin surrounding the metal plate was smooth as though the disk had always been a part of him. In the center of the plate was a small keyhole.

Her touch always sent shivers through his body, and even the insertion of the tiny skeleton key was sensual. He closed his eyes as she began to rotate the key in a clockwise direction. He wondered if the cylindrical metal box inside his chest felt cold the way metal usually did, or was it warm from his body? From her nearness. He sensed her fingers brushing his chest. He could feel the clicking of the small wheels and gears deep within and imagined the mainspring tightening.

She finished and buttoned his shirt, blushing as she always did.

"My turn?" he asked quite innocently.

"Mr. Thackery, you are so predictable. Or should I say despicable."

She turned away from him and once she was sure no one else was in the vicinity, undid one stay on her dress. The disk in her own chest was silver to match the tiny key she bore around her neck in its simplicity. She inserted her key into the disk positioned perfectly between her breasts. With her own hand, she turned the tiny crank positioned in the center of the cleft of the heart.

He swore he could hear the clicks and imagined his own fingers turning the key, his hand so close to the warmth of her body. Henry sighed, hoping they could live forever, so this communion between them could be repeated again and again. And at some point, even if it took another a hundred years, he felt sure his fingers would someday turn that key.

The Present

Henry pulled his coat tighter about him as a breeze from the lake reached with wintry fingers to claw at them. The sycamore tree, now over a hundred years old, appeared skeleton-like, its leaves having scattered weeks earlier. Its bare branches provided little cover to the park bench as the threat of a winter storm loomed on the horizon.

Though Henry could not recall the tree being planted, he could still appreciate its sturdiness and beauty. He watched as two doves huddled in its branches. Well, they may have been pigeons, but Henry preferred to think of them as doves.

"I rented the newest movie version of *Around the World in 80 Days* last night," he confided.

She smiled. "Do you mean to tell me you have still not read the book?"

He reached into his tattered briefcase and pulled out the leather-bound copy of the book Emily had given him nearly seventy-five years earlier. It had rarely been out of his possession. "I have not yet, my dear lady. It is much too elegant for reading. It is a treasure I am saving."

"No doubt you're right about that. It's a first edition, Henry," Emily reminded him. "Probably worth a fortune by now."

Henry shrugged. "Perhaps I will pick up a used paperback version the next time I visit Goodwill."

She laughed. "Henry, you are one of the richest men in America and still you browse in secondhand stores. You might also be the strangest man in America. But secondhand stores?"

"How do you think I remained rich?"

"If you are so frugal, why do you insist on buying me expensive gifts?"

"Emily! The true treasure of my life is not wealth nor contraptions nor things—but *you*. Why should I not shower you with expressions of my deep adoration?"

"Well, by now you should have grown tired of returning them each time I sent them back! Or do you have your secretary return them for you?"

"Who said I return them?"

She gazed into his eyes. Henry knew she could not tell if he was serious or not. He smiled, and his fingers touched the vest pocket that held his key and the ring. The ring he had kept there for over a century.

"So I assume you brought another gift today?"

He shrugged. "Perhaps, as you say, I have tired of returning them." She looked disappointed.

"But maybe not."

She brightened. She wouldn't accept the gift, of course, but he knew his presentation of them to her had become an exciting ritual. "Just no more cars, please! That's what started all of this! Surely, Henry, you remember that day."

And this time he did.

1925

"What do you think?" Henry asked, settling onto the park bench next to Emily.

"About what, my dear Henry? The weather? The Charleston? *The Great Gatsby*?"

"What in heaven's name is a *gatsby*?"

"Henry Thackery! How do you ever expect to be a truly educated man, to say nothing of a contemporary man, if you never read? *The Great Gatsby* is the newest book by F. Scott Fitzgerald. I believe it captures the startling culture of this generation. And how can you expect to be a good business man if you are behind in the popular culture of the times, Henry?"

"I wasn't expecting a lecture on literature, my dear, nor did I request business advice, though I'm grateful for your interest in my welfare. I inquired what you think about the motor vehicle parked over there near the curb."

She took a good look at the car from front fender to rear taillights. "Looks like the new Packard Runabout, I believe. Very nice. I like the red paint job, but I don't think it suits you."

"No, but *you* would look very sporting behind the wheel," he said, dangling a set of keys before her.

Emily lifted a hand to her mouth to stifle a gasp. "Henry, I could never—"

"Please, Emily. It would do my heart good."

She laughed. "There is nothing I can do that can improve your heart, Henry. And while I admire the car—and I love the thought behind your gesture—I cannot accept such an extravagant gift." She stiffened her resolve and looked him straight in the eye. "I refuse to be beholden to you or anyone else. I was...*kept*, once. My late husband, while I loved him dearly, near the end, he—" She stopped short, casting her gaze downward. "Never mind. I cannot accept the gift."

"You won't even take a closer look at it?" he asked.

"I dare not," she replied. "I would be too afraid of falling in love with it. Then what would I do except mourn the loss when someone else drives it away."

The disappointment on his face was easy to read as a slight frown tugged at his wrinkles. He sighed deeply, and she touched his hand. "But I do have a gift for you," she said as she pulled a leather-bound book from her satchel. "It is an English first edition of *Around the World in 80 Days*."

He took the book from her hands, running his fingers over the fine leather. "And even though you have rejected all my gifts, you expect me to accept this gift from you?"

She nodded.

He had to agree. The book was the perfect gift. It was personal and well thought out. The expensive, shiny Packard was... well, it was just an automobile. He scolded himself and accepted the book without protest.

"Thank you, Emily. I shall treasure it forever."

"I would rather you actually opened it up and read it sometime."

Henry smiled, slipping the Verne novel into his new briefcase.

Emily touched his sleeve. "Perhaps if you have brought us a nice lunch today, I will allow you and your driver to take me back to my shop when we are done. What did you bring today?"

A look of alarm filled his face, widening his green eyes. "I thought it was your turn."

She feigned a frown until he reached into his briefcase and pulled out two thick sandwiches wrapped in butcher paper.

"I know how you love a Rueben sandwich," he said with a broad smile.

She laughed, and they ate their leisurely lunch as the small sycamore tree near their bench entertained a robin that swooped down to a low-hanging bow to feed her nest of baby birds.

"I like your new hat," she said, dabbing her mouth with a cloth napkin. "It's a new style, isn't it?"

"It's called a Homburg," he said with pride.

"I like it better than that silly bowler. Much more dignified, I think."

"Thank you, my lady," he said, tipping the brim to her. "And I must say, your new outfit is wonderful. Did you make it yourself?"

She nodded and smoothed the skirt of her empire-waisted, pink and yellow chintz dress with a flattering pattern of pink *fleur de lis* trim around the bust. "I fashioned it after the newest line from Paris. It is probably much too young for me and perhaps a bit too daring as well."

He glanced at her cleavage, but it hadn't been the first time he had done so that day. The new dress amplified her bust nicely. She was usually much more conservative. She pretended not to notice the direction of his glance.

"It is very becoming," he said.

She blushed and took her time folding her napkin into a precise square. She gazed out over the rippling waters of the lake and was silent for quite some time.

"A penny for your thoughts?" he asked as the silence finally got to him.

"*Un sou pour vos pensées?*"

"I beg your pardon?"

"It is French for 'a penny for your thoughts,' my dear," she explained. "Really, Henry. I cannot imagine how you've managed to acquire such wealth in your life without acquiring any wealth in your head! Don't you know any language other than American English?"

"I think everything sounds much more eloquent in French," he mused. "But I suspect that would hardly be the case should I try to speak the language."

"It has been called 'the language of love' in case you didn't know."

"Well. In that case, I suppose I had better learn it."

She laughed softly. "In order to learn to speak the language, you might actually have to read a book or two in French."

"Not necessarily," he countered. "I could hire a tutor."

"A beautiful French one perhaps?"

"Perhaps. Are you available for lessons?"

"Ah, but I am not French, monsieur."

"Maybe not, but you are certainly beautiful."

She blushed again. "Your eyesight must be failing you, Henry. I'm getting rather old. Unless you forgot, my birthday is next month. My goodness. I'll be 82."

"And yet, you have the figure of a Greek goddess."

"And have you actually met any Greek goddesses to support this claim? Your fibs grow grander every year, Henry."

A horn blared in the distance. The street that bordered the park wasn't as quiet as it had been a quarter of a century earlier.

"I asked you about your thoughts, Emily, and you still haven't answered my question," he reminded her. "I've known you for nearly half a century, and I know when something is bothering you. Is Kathleen well?"

Emily nodded. "My daughter is fine, Henry. Thank you for asking. She can, however, be most irritating at times because she keeps asking why we haven't married yet."

"Well, that shows she is smart enough to realize, as I have, that there is no logical reason that we should not be wed. But you still have failed to answer the question I ask every week. Why do you avoid answering me, my dear?"

Emily hesitated. "Because I have to know, Henry."

"Emily, you know. You know I love you. You know I want to marry you and take care of you. And, yes, you know I'd love to see you without a stitch of clothing on."

"Henry!"

"Sorry. I didn't mean to make light of your concerns, whatever they may be. Please tell me what you feel you need to know."

"The question. The question that has stayed with me for years," she said, but it seemed to Henry almost as if she were talking to herself. "Why was I chosen to receive this heart?" she continued. "It has preyed on my mind since the day I signed the papers consenting to the operation. The physicians refused to tell me the identity of my benefactor, and why such an expensive, experimental process should be undertaken on behalf of a middle-class, widowed shop girl! They told me I should be grateful for the opportunity. One even said that it was God smiling on me, but I think perhaps it wasn't God. And over the years, I have come to believe that the choice of me as the recipient wasn't merely scientific, either. I believe someone, some mysterious benefactor, chose me and paid for the procedure."

She eyed him warily. "I can't imagine how or why anyone would take such an interest in me. I had no friends outside of my late husband's, and none of them had the means or the inclination to pay for such an extravagance. I only wish I knew who purchased this heart for me! It has weighed on me ever since I made the decision to accept."

"Do you regret accepting the procedure?" he asked.

She hesitated for a moment. "Sometimes, perhaps. Originally, I accepted the gift for my daughter, you know. She'd already lost her father. I couldn't bear the thought of her being orphaned at so tender an age."

Henry nodded knowingly. "But perhaps some things are better left unknown, Emily. You are alive and in good health. You have enjoyed many wonderful years with your daughter, her children, and now, her children's children. It seems to me like that should be enough, and you should be grateful for that."

"It is not that I am ungrateful, but the longer I live, the more urgent it becomes to me to discover the truth. Each year that passes, my heart never falters. Nearly everyone I knew as a girl has passed on, and other than you and my daughter's lineage, I am alone in this world. Most likely, the person who paid for my heart is no longer alive and would not care if the secret were kept or not. Certainly enough time has passed that any medical records regarding the procedure should be available to the public."

"If any such records survived. It has been half a century."

She continued. "I'm thinking about hiring an investigator!"

"An investigator! But why? I don't understand why this knowledge is so important to you," Henry said. "Perhaps you were the first to receive the heart. Perhaps the doctor who invented it wanted to test his contraption on a beautiful woman. Perhaps the hospital received a legacy from some wealthy patient who'd passed on declaring that it be used to help a middleclass shop girl. There are so many possibilities, Emily."

"Perhaps—"

"And what could an investigator learn, Emily? Nearly fifty years have passed. Half the doctors and nurses on that medical staff have undoubtedly passed on. And remember, the procedure was so dangerous to human life it was outlawed. It is highly conceivable that all the documentation of our procedures was ordered destroyed in order to prevent future attempts of the surgery. It seems like a waste of time to me."

She sighed. "You're probably right. But I do not sleep well at night just thinking about it."

"Perhaps you would sleep better with a husband in your bed," he suggested.

She laughed softly. "Oh, have you a husband in mind?"

"Well, there is that homeless vagrant camping out down by the railroad tracks. I've not seen his face—only smelled him, really—but he certainly seems in need of a wife," Henry suggested, pulling a fresh cigar from his coat pocket. He clipped the end and struck a match. His hand shook slightly as he placed a match to the tip of the cigar and puffed.

She usually commented on the odor, but her gaze was distant this day. He watched her as he enjoyed his smoke in silence and saw her withdraw a small bag of bread from her purse to feed the ducks waddling to their bench.

Emily finally reached down and pulled her key from the swooping neckline of her dress. She looked at him, an unasked question in her eyes. Finally, she said, "It's time. I must be getting back to my shop, Henry."

She played with the weight of the key and chain in her hand for a moment as she looked up at him. Reservation held her mouth in a thin pink line, but after a moment, she sighed. "Oh, Henry. You really are just an innocent, are you not?" She looked at him imploringly.

He remained silent.

She searched his face for a long moment, and then her shoulders seemed to sink. With an almost imperceptible nod, she lowered her hand to Henry's and upturned his palm. She released her key into his hand and looked down at the ground beside her.

"Will you wind my heart, Henry?"

If Henry's heart could fly—and perhaps with the attachment of mechanical wings, it could—Henry would have been hovering in the sky above them then, coasting on a cloud. A grateful smile lifted the corners of his mouth.

He nodded and retrieved his own key as well. "And will you wind mine? Shall we do them together?"

Her eyes brightened for a moment, the hint of a smile lingering on her lips. "Yes," she said. Simultaneously, they pushed their keys into the lock plates of each other's breast and turned slowly.

Henry turned the key between his fingers more slowly than Emily, savoring the moment that he had waited for, for such a long time. He grazed his fingertips lightly over the smooth, peachy skin of her breast as he turned the key. The clicking seemed to grow tighter before finally the spring released and the mechanical heart was fully wound. With a sigh, he removed the key and slowly withdrew his fingers from her chest.

"Thank you," she said, returning his key to him. She held her palm out, and with a slight hesitation, he dropped her key into her waiting hand.

Another horn blared in the distance as a gust of wind detached a few dozen leaves from the sycamore tree near their bench. The autumn leaves danced before them, putting on a colorful performance, but neither of them noticed.

When Emily rose from the bench, she took a step forward so that Henry could no longer see her face and said, "Someday I'll find out the truth, Henry. And that truth is the most important thing to me in this world." She took a breath. "Indeed, Henry. I imagine that someday, it will be all I have left."

The Present

The snowfall increased as Henry tried to shut out the blare of traffic outside the park. Although his hearing was not as good as it used to be, the clamor bothered him more than ever.

"Are you warm enough?" he asked, returning his leather-bound Jules Verne to his briefcase where it would be protected from the weather.

"I'm fine."

"Perhaps we should go back to my place and share a snifter of brandy or some Port."

"No, thank you, Henry. The snow is so beautiful. Let's enjoy it awhile longer, shall we?" She gave his hand a squeeze. "Did I ever thank you, Henry?"

"For what?"

"You know what I'm talking about."

And he did.

1950

It was hot that summer. Hotter than Henry could remember in recent years. He was wearing his three-piece Italian suit as he had just come from a business meeting, but he wished he had changed into something cooler. On the other hand, he always liked to look his best for Emily.

He withdrew his pocket watch from his vest and flicked it open. The watch had been in his possession some eighty years and still kept perfect time. Looking at it, he realized suddenly that it was most likely nearly a match for the inner workings of his heart. He snapped the cover closed and slipped the timepiece back into the pocket on his vest. A pocket holding the few things he still considered precious after all these years—his watch, his key, and the ring.

He began to worry.

Emily hadn't missed a lunch date in, well—he couldn't even recall the last time.

Had a customer kept her busy at the shop?

Henry wasn't sure why she still kept the business open after all these years. She could have retired long ago. Of course, people could say the same about him.

Had she fallen ill?

Were her grandchildren okay?

Her daughter had passed away nearly a decade earlier, and Emily had been devastated for weeks. And her grandchildren weren't exactly young. But even then, Emily still made their weekly lunch together, grief-stricken as she was.

Just as Henry made the decision to walk the few blocks to her shop, she appeared through the trees. Her walk was measured, and at one point, he could have sworn she almost turned back.

She carried no picnic basket.

Something was wrong.

Emily approached the bench but did not sit down.

Henry swore his heart skipped a beat, but he knew that was impossible.

Emily stood before him for what felt like an eternity until a tear rolled down her face.

"Emily?"

"Don't say a word, you bastard!"

Henry was shocked. In the seventy-five years he had known her, he had never heard her utter a profanity.

Emily pulled a lace handkerchief from a dress pocket and wiped away the tear. "I knew it, too. Somehow, I always knew it, but I rationalized it away. It couldn't be. I hadn't even met you until after— after—Oh, how could you? Why didn't you tell me? Why did you lie to me, Henry?"

"Calm down, Emily. Please sit for a moment." Henry remained seated.

"I will not calm down, Henry Thackery! Do not command me as if you own me! You might own my heart in some sense, but you do not own me and you certainly do not own my soul."

"Emily—"

She wiped away another tear.

Her voice dropped to barely a whisper. "Why didn't you tell me you paid for my heart? I gave you every opportunity. Every possible window. You scoundrel! You knew how much it bothered me. How could you not admit the truth?"

Henry felt like a cat cornered by a wild-eyed dog frothing at the mouth.

Her eyes never seemed to blink as they bored into him.

He also felt like a fool.

After a moment, he began, "I didn't tell you because I didn't know how you would take it. All these years you have refused every gift I have ever offered. If you knew that I had given you this gift, something you would see as more extravagant, perhaps, than any other, well—I was afraid if you found out, I might lose you. I love you, Emily. I've loved you since the first time I saw you. And when I overheard the doctors say you had only weeks left—"

"How could you have loved me then, Henry? You didn't even know me."

"I don't pretend to understand the mysteries of love, Emily. In fact, I had never truly been in love before the day I met you. And I certainly did not believe in love at first sight—until that very moment."

"Do you have any idea what I've been through? My husband, he paid a dowry for me without my even knowing it. Can you imagine that? I'd never even met him, and there it was, a price paid in full to my father like I was some piece of livestock. And I had to go away with him, had to live with him and be his wife because he *paid for me*, Henry. I guess you simply get used to it as time passes. There is someone there to care for. Someone to have a child with. Someone to grow old with. I suppose I loved him in some way. Especially after our daughter was born, but I swore on his grave that I would never be beholden to another man for the rest of my life, Henry. Never! And look what you have done. You have purchased my heart! You have *bought* me my life."

Henry looked at her pleadingly, his hands turned upward in a gesture of begging. He was helpless. He was silent.

"You should have told me, Henry," she said coldly.

And with that, she turned and walked away.

He did not try to stop her.

He simply sat there.

Was it his imagination, or had the birds stopped singing in the nearby sycamore tree and were the usually playful squirrels nowhere to be found?

Stan Swanson

Winter was on its way.

Henry's hand rose to his breast pocket and lingered over the ring hidden there. It was a princess-cut diamond set against two emeralds in platinum. A fine ring for a fine woman, who would likely never wear it now. He finally withdrew his key and sat for quite some time, rolling it between his fingers, debating whether or not to actually use it. Despite the steady sound of the ticking inside his chest, he was sure his heart was broken beyond repair.

The wind blew steadily colder.

The Present

"No, my dear, Henry. I don't believe I ever did thank you," Emily said, squeezing his hand. He curled his fingers around hers.

"Well, you certainly didn't want to thank me that particular day. I didn't think I would ever see you again, Emily. I may be getting forgetful in my old age, but that is a day I shall never forget. You know, I never told you this, but I almost didn't wind my heart that day."

The abrupt intake of her breath seemed unnaturally loud.

"Henry! You're not serious! You're such a strong, determined person! How could you have even considered such a thing? I am so sorry."

"You have nothing to be sorry about, my dear. It was I who withheld that secret from you for so long."

She reached out and brushed a few snowflakes from his overcoat. "It doesn't matter now, Henry. We're alive, and the day is grand. It makes one feel so full of life, doesn't it? I love watching the snowfall, don't you? It's so peaceful. So quiet."

Henry thought his idea of brandy near a warm, cozy fire sounded better, but he didn't say a word. If Emily had suggested they simply sit there and freeze to death, he would have considered it. He fastened the top button of his coat and wished he had brought his leather gloves.

The weather continued to worsen.

"Henry—"

He turned to look at her, the tone in her voice catching his attention immediately. "Yes, my dear?"

"I saw my doctor this morning."

He blinked a snowflake from his eye. "Fit as a fiddle?"

She didn't answer, but shook her head.

"Is everything all right, Emily? It's not your heart, is it?"

"Of course not," she said with a small smile. "This stupid old heart is going to beat forever."

He was afraid to voice the question that hung in the air, but he didn't have to.

"Henry," she said, squeezing his hand more firmly. "I have cancer—"

The swirling snow made the statement more ominous. And Henry wasn't nearly as cold as he had been a moment earlier.

1975

Leaves of yellow, gold, red, and orange danced around Henry's feet as he shuffled along the path. He held his worn briefcase in one hand and a hand-carved cane in the other.

The cane had been an expensive gift from some Japanese businessman whose name he could not recall. He had placed it in a dusty closet corner some thirty years earlier and nearly forgotten about it until recently. The briefcase had been a Christmas gift from Emily. It had been "gently used" when she had given it to him and now carried the scars of an additional fifty years.

There was little doubt which he treasured more.

He despised the cane, not because of whom had given it to him, but because he now needed to use it. He was thankful, however, that he had not reached the point of requiring one of those confounded walkers he had seen in the nursing home near his brownstone. He did, however, need the cane for keeping his balance. Emily thought it gave him character. He thought it made him look like an old man.

His heart might be nearly indestructible, but other body parts seemed envious of the Merganthol Circulatory Assistance Device and rebelled in their own fashion, refusing to react as they had years earlier.

Henry approached the new metal bench and settled into place. He much preferred the worn wooden one, which had served them for many years. He had even written to the city to complain about how uncomfortable the new benches were and how cold they got in the winter. He had even offered to pay for new wooden benches, but he never received a reply.

A gaggle of Canadian geese flew in formation over the water of the lake as Emily approached. Her lively gait made him feel like an old man. Was 112 considered old when you had a heart that would never fail, he wondered? In any event, he placed his cane to the side opposite where she would sit, so that it would be less conspicuous to her.

Emily had aged incredibly well. Although she no longer troubled to dye her once-upon-a-time flaxen hair, she still looked grand. He himself loved the pure silver color and complained when she had cut it short for the summer.

Henry considered himself the luckiest man in the universe for having known her all these years and the unluckiest for never having convinced her to become his wife.

"Henry," she said as she sat down. "You look wonderful today. The nip of autumn in the air suits you well."

He tipped his new Panama hat.

"I don't find dishonesty a desirable trait in my women, but I believe I will make an exception in this case."

She chuckled. "*Your* women? I gather then that you have hoards of them stashed around the city?"

He laughed. "Oh, most certainly! But please don't convey that information to Emily Harding, the dear lady that she is. She would be overly jealous, I am afraid."

"Perhaps," Emily answered. "But then again, I hear she has a harem of Armenian lovers secreted around the city, one or two Amazonian adventurers, and a British secret agent as well."

"Oh, I think not, my lady. Emily Harding is a most virtuous woman whose righteousness is only matched by her intelligence and beauty."

Emily placed two fingers over his lips to silence him, and he tenderly kissed them.

She smiled and drew those same fingers down his clean-shaven chin.

"I miss your goatee," she said.

"And I miss your long hair," he replied.

"Touché."

A single leaf of gold and brown fluttered into her lap like some rare species of butterfly. She picked it up gently as if she could bring it back to life or at least comfort it as it faded away.

"Winter's just around the corner, Henry."

He made a sound indicating his displeasure.

"I hate winter."

"But still you insist on meeting me here every week, rain or shine."

"Call me sentimental," he said. "But we could move to Miami. Or at least migrate to the south in the winter as the more sensible species do. I've always thought of having a winter home in a warmer climate."

"My home is here, Henry. You know that. And my grandchildren are here. Who would look after them?"

"They should be looking after you," he replied.

"You're probably right. It vexes me that at times they seem older and more invalid than I."

"I don't believe I've ever heard anyone use the word 'vex' in a sentence since 1912, I think," he said, attempting to lighten her mood.

"How about the word 'exasperate,' Henry. Have you ever heard that one used more recently?" He got the point.

"How did your doctor's appointment go?" he asked.

"Fine," she replied. "He increased my thyroid medicine. He also wants to schedule a mammogram, a chest x-ray, and a couple of other humiliating procedures I'd rather not discuss. But other than that, he pronounced me fit as a fiddle. And, yes, he actually used those words."

"I concur with his assessment," Henry said with a grin. "Your body looks especially fine to me. Did he get to see you naked?"

"Henry! How can you still make me blush after all these years?"

"Well," he answered. "I can assure you that there are certain things you do that make certain body parts of mine react as well, though maybe not as urgently as earlier days."

"Henry!"

He grinned.

"And what did the doctor say about your heart?"

"What would he say? The same thing he says every year. I think he is obsessed with it. He still marvels at the thing and wonders how they accomplished such an amazing medical procedure in what he considers to be the Dark Ages. He goes on and on about how my indestructible heart came out of a time when madness was treated with electrical shocks and colds were managed with leeches. Sometimes I think he hopes he'll still be around when I die just so he can dissect me."

"I think you read too much Poe," Henry replied.

"Nobody today writes anything as good or as scary as Poe or Lovecraft," she replied. "These modern day writers don't know how to draft a good thrill. Oh, did *60 Minutes* approach you? They said they were going to. I turned down the interview, of course."

He nodded. "I told them if they contacted me again, I'd send my lawyers after them."

"It seems like every other decade, we're suddenly a breaking news story. Every time my great-grandchild mentions her grammy's magical heart or when some nurse at the medical center sees me changing into one of those ridiculous gowns. Even now, I occasionally feel like a display at the circus when people find out who I am. It's as if I'm one of those sensational news stories they make up to fill the pages in those yellow tabloids. You know. Like a headline that reads, 'Three-Headed Cow Gives Birth to an Alien from Neptune' or 'Elvis is a Robot' or some other ridiculous story."

A breeze materialized from the north, and a few more colored leaves trickled down, joining their companions in the yellowed grass beneath the sycamore tree.

"Roger Hennessey died last month," she said softly.

He nodded. "I heard. Brain aneurism. Guess that leaves—what, four of us?"

"Three," she replied. "Charles Culbertson died this past summer as well. Automobile accident."

"Well, at least it wasn't their hearts."

"Henry, how can you be so callous?"

"Must be old age creeping up on me."

"I don't believe it crept up on you, Mr. Thackery. I believe it hit you head on and slammed you against a wall."

He ignored the remark as there were certain topics he found were arguments not worth the battle.

""Maybe it's time we took a vacation now that we're both retired. Switzerland has nice mountains. And I hear Peru is wonderful this time of year."

"Peru? I haven't been out of the city in decades, Henry. Don't be ridiculous! And why Peru? Why not Oklahoma or Kansas?"

He wasn't sure if she was being facetious or not. Knowing a woman for nearly a hundred years didn't necessarily mean you were allowed to see the inner workings of her mind. It was a lesson he had eventually—and painstakingly—learned over the years.

"Kansas?"

"Sure. Why not? Maybe I'd like to see the house where Dorothy lived before I climb a Peruvian mountain."

"Dorothy?" Now he was completely befuddled. "You mean, like in *The Wizard of Oz*? We saw that at the RKO in the early '40s, I believe. Remember?"

She sighed. "Yes, Henry, I remember. It was 1939 to be precise. It was also a book before it was a movie. And, no, there's no Dorothy house in Kansas except for the one they built to replicate the one in the film."

"And you want to visit this house?"

"Henry, Henry, Henry—" She gave him a peck on the forehead. "How can such an intelligent man be so ignorant at times?"

Henry chewed on the inside of his cheek. "I take it that is a rhetorical question?" A gust of wind sailed through the park and played briefly with the leaves before moving on. He took a deep breath.

"I have a gift for you—" he began.

She frowned. "Henry, you know I only accept gifts on my birthday and at Christmas."

He smiled wryly. "There was a time when you wouldn't even do that."

"Regardless, the holidays are still far off, and it certainly isn't my birthday—unless your addled brain has forgotten the date."

"I remember when your birthday is," he replied. "I haven't lost my memory quite yet. But I think you'll like this."

She groaned as he handed her a package tied with a bright red ribbon and a neatly tied bow. "Well, at least you went to the trouble of having it gift wrapped," she said.

"I wrapped it myself," he said softly.

Her hands froze in midair above the ribbon. "You did this, Henry? Why, it is beautiful!"

"Took me nearly three hours," he muttered, though he was secretly delighted with the compliment. "You should see my parlor. Ribbon scattered from one end to the other."

She chuckled. The scene was easily imaginable.

Slowly, as if to savor every second, Emily carefully pulled the ribbon from the package and tucked it neatly into her purse as if it were the actual gift. She was just as careful with the wrapping, and as she pulled the paper open, she gasped. A tear came to her eye, and she snatched a tissue from her bag.

"Emily?" His inquiry was tentative. He did not like to see her so emotional. Especially when he was unsure of the reason. Was she angry? Pleased? She turned and kissed him full on the lips, and although that wasn't the first time she had done so, it certainly felt that way. Her lips lingered and slowly withdrew.

"I will treasure it forever," she said, holding the old book in her hands.

She had somehow misplaced her copy years ago.

"Is it the right one?" he asked.

She opened the cover. "A first edition. Oh, Henry, how did you ever find it?"

She closed the cover and ran her fingers over the gilded title.

"*Around the World in 80 Days.*" She kissed him once again. "And in the original French. Thank you, Henry. It is the most wonderful gift I have ever received." And she kissed him once more for good measure.

"If I had known I'd receive this kind of reaction, I would have given you a book every week I've known you."

She smiled. "This isn't just any book, Henry, and you know it." Another gust of wind whipped around them, and she shivered.

He removed his topcoat, and she gladly accepted it as he wrapped it about her shoulders.

She laid her head briefly on his shoulder, and as he reached into his vest pocket—past the ring that had resided there for years—he removed the key. They had used it so many times over the years. It was beginning to show signs of wear. It made it that much more special.

He handed her the key. She accepted without hesitation, their fingers lingering as they touched. Just as he had done a thousand times before, he unfastened the center button of his shirt and revealed the shiny, untarnished gold that had become as much a part of his being as the toes on his feet.

Emily touched the circular plate with a slight caress and slowly slid the key into place. She turned it gently, and the soft clicking could even be heard over the rising wind. With one last turn, she removed the key and pressed it back into his hand.

She then removed the silver chain from around her neck and

handed it to Henry. It was warm to the touch, retaining the heat from her body.

He felt something of a voyeur as she pulled open the topcoat he had draped about her and undid the top button of her blouse. After a quick glance around the immediate vicinity, she undid a second button, revealing the twin of his disk, nestled between her breasts just above her lacy white brassiere.

She closed her eyes.

Holding the key tightly, he lowered his head and kissed the disk, then gently ran his lips over the swell of her breasts. She took a deep breath, her eyes remaining shut. He drew a circle around the silver disk with the key, then slid it tenderly into the center of the disk. He then softly caressed her breasts beneath her bra with one hand as he turned the key with the other.

Click.

Click.

He withdrew the key and with one last kiss between her breasts, rebuttoned her blouse. They sat there for several moments, the cool wind not feeling as cold as it had earlier.

"You are quite the quixotic figure, Henry."

"Is that good or bad?" he asked, handing her back the chain and the key to her heart.

"It is a wonderful thing, Henry. You make me feel young and beautiful. That is a grand thing for an old woman."

He smiled.

"You are beautiful."

She laughed. "Did you forget to bring your glasses again?"

But he would not be so easily disregarded. "I have one last gift," he said, the nervousness apparent in his voice.

"Henry—"

"Will you finally accept me? I may never offer it again if you do not."

With that, he withdrew the shiny engagement ring from his vest pocket, and before she could stop him, he groaned to a kneel before her on the gravel path.

"Please, Henry," she begged. "We have been through this so many times. And it has been such a wonderful day. Don't spoil it for me."

He ignored her. "Emily Louise Harding. Will you do me the pleasure of being my wife?"

A tear rolled down her cheek.

"Henry—"

He ran a hand through his thinning gray hair and smiled even though he knew her answer.

"Not today, Henry. I love you dearly, but I cannot. I am old. You are old. We have lived separate lives for years and have little in common. What would you do all day while I read my novels? Would you set up a train track in the attic? Perhaps collect stamps or coins from around the world? Maybe you would finally buy a television set and watch westerns and detective shows every night."

"Maybe I could start a gift-wrapping service."

She managed a small smile. "Would you go with me to the opera?" she asked.

"Of course I would."

"Would you enjoy it?"

"Probably not."

"Would you go with me while I spend countless hours browsing through libraries and bookstores?"

"Most certainly."

"Would you enjoy it?"

"Perhaps not, my dear Emily, but I would enjoy the fact that I was with you regardless of where we might be or what we might be doing."

"I'm sorry, Henry. Please forgive me. I cannot marry someone just for the sake of marriage. I am not interested in being kept, nor am I interested in having someone follow me around like a lost puppy dog unable to enjoy anything around him. It would ruin us, Henry."

She pushed his hand away, and he returned the ring to the safety of his vest pocket. He then reached out and wiped a tear from Emily's cheek.

"No rush," he said quietly. "I'll try again in another twenty-five years or so."

She brushed her fingers through the hair he had mussed and kissed the top of his head.

"Will you please get off your knees? You're getting your trousers filthy, and those squirrels are giving us strange looks."

He grinned. "I've been trying to get up for the last five minutes, my dear. Will you please hand me my blasted cane?"

The wind off the lake picked up, causing the multicolored leaves to dance about their bench like pixies in some enchanted glen.

A quarter of a century—

Not so long, he told himself. Not long at all. Simply a blink in the eye of time.

The Present

"Cancer?"

He could not comprehend her statement, no matter how he tried. He thought his heart would stop right then and there, but the steady *click* seemed louder than ever. She reached for his hand and held it tightly.

"How long?" he asked in a voice so strained he did not recognize it.

"A few weeks," she said as if she were simply discussing the weather.

"No. Absolutely not! I cannot accept that! We will find the finest doctors in the city. In the world! Money is no object. Emily—we have to fight this!"

She squeezed his hand. "Henry, there is nothing to be done. It was discovered too late."

They sat there in the deserted park for quite some time. The snow began collecting on the cement pathway, sucking the warmth from the ground. Henry and Emily did not notice as the hazy winter sun fell to midpoint in the sky.

"Emily?"

She snuggled close to him as much for comfort as for warmth.

"Yes, my dear?"

He opened his hand and revealed the engagement ring he had carried and offered so many times.

She closed her eyes. Henry was afraid that if she cried, her tears might turn to ice. Or even worse, that he himself might cry. Emily opened her eyes again, and tears did flow, but they were accompanied by a tender smile. She held out her left hand, and ever so slowly, Henry slid the ring onto her finger.

She reached into his vest pocket, and her fingers tightened around the key, which dwelled within. She unbuttoned his shirt and upon inserting the key, wound his heart slowly. With each whisper of a clock, a tear ran down her face.

"I love you, Emily Harding."

"And I love you, Henry Thackery. With all my heart."

He reached for the chain around her neck, but she closed her hand over his, and she gently pushed it away.

"You only have about twenty minutes, Emily. I should wind your heart for you."

"I am dying, Henry."

"But you are not dying today!" he replied, pressing on.

"I would rather choose the time and the place, my dearest Henry. And I choose it to be here and now at this cherished spot with the person I've loved for more years than I care to count."

"Emily—"

"Do not argue with me, my sweet. It will do you no good. I have lived a good, fulfilling life. And longer than a person should, I now believe. Hold me close, Henry Thackery, but let me go as well..."

He kissed her gently on the lips, and they sat huddled for quite some time. Snow gathered over them, dusting their coats. After a while, it began to collect on their faces. Henry looked at Emily from the corner of his eye She looked like she was decorated with diamonds as the snow glistened on her cheeks and nose. For quite some time, they sat listening to the quiet clicks of their hearts, sometimes in harmony, sometimes in counter beats. And then, after a time, only one heart continued to click.

Softly.

Lonely.

Henry kissed her lightly on her mouth, still faintly warm though her spirit had already floated from her body. Carefully, he moved his fingertips over her eyelids, pressing them softly closed.

He drew a finger over the key to his own heart in the palm of his hand. A tear streamed down his cheek, cold, as it cut a swath through the already melting layer of snow that sprinkled his skin.

Closing his eyes tightly to stop the flow of tears, he gripped both keys in his palm, and without hesitation, he flung them through the air and watched as they made a quiet splash into the wintry water of the lake.

The snow continued to fall, quietly and peacefully, as the two indestructible hearts finally broke.

Acknowledgements

Wind Up Hearts was written several years ago and has undergone many changes since that original version. It was previously published by Curiosity Quills Press as an e-book as well as one of the entries in their *Chronology* anthology. I've always wanted to see it in paperback format and, finally, the time has come. (It will also be republished in e-book format.) I especially want to thank my wife, Joy, for her suggestions after reading the story many times. Araminta Star Matthews and Jennifer Word also provided me with many suggestions and words of encouragement along the way. I would also be amiss if I didn't mention the great pre-publication editing skills of Frances (Franny) Hogg Lochow.

About the Author

Stan Swanson is a Bram Stoker award finalist and author of ten books including *Forever Zombie* (a collection of short stories), *Write of the Living Dead* (a highly-praised writing guide written with Araminta Star Matthews and Rachel Lee) and *Return of the Scream Queen* (co-authored with Michael McCarty and Linnea Quigley). He was also the founder of Dark Moon Books and *Dark Moon Digest*.

TITLES BY STAN SWANSON
Inspiration for Songwriters
The Songwriter's Journal
Dragontooth: The Prequel
Forever Zombie
The Misadventures of Hobart Hucklebuck: Magic & Mayhem
The Misadventures of Hobart Hucklebuck: Pandemonium in Pennywhistle
Return of the Scream Queen
(with Michael McCarty and Linnea Quigley)
Horror High School: Return of the Loving Dead
(with Araminta Star Matthews)
Write of the Living Dead
(with Araminta Star Matthews and Rachel Lee)

IN THE WORKS
The Methlands: A Novel
Real Vampires Don't Eat Quiche
(First book in the Zander Cross almost-cozy mystery series)